Childrens Press International
Distributed by Childrens Press, Chicago.
1987 School and Library Edition

Library of Congress Cataloging-in-Publication Data

Mahy, Margaret.
    The man who enjoyed grumbling.

    Summary: When the Goat family moves to get away
from their grumbly neighbor Mr. Ratchett, they miss
having someone to tease and he misses having something
to complain about.
    [1. Goats—Fiction 2. Neighborliness—Fiction]
I. Hodder, Wendy, ill. II. Title.
PZ7.M2773Mak   1987   [E]   87-845
ISBN 0-516-08971-4

Created and Designed by Wendy Pye, Ltd.

The Man Who
Enjoyed Grumbling

CHILDRENS PRESS INTERNATIONAL

Scratchy Mr. Ratchet
enjoyed a good grumble.
He got plenty of practice
because he lived next door
to the Goat family.

The Goat family liked making trouble.
They bunted and bleated.
They nibbled his hedge.
Sometimes they put their horns down
and chased his cat.

It didn't matter.
Scratchy Mr. Ratchett
enjoyed having something
to grumble about.

2

One day,
he put on his grumpy gardening clothes
and his special moaning boots
and went out to garden and grumble.

What was this?
Things were very quiet.
Things were too quiet.
Mr. Ratchett looked over the hedge.
He saw a moving van.
The Goats' grandfather clock
was being loaded into it
by two moving men.
Then the men loaded
the Goats' television set.

4

"Where are you taking that television set?"
shouted scratchy Mr. Ratchett.

"The Goat family has moved
up into the high hills,"
said one of the moving men.

"They wanted a place with more room
for jumping around,"
said the other moving man.

"What nonsense!
They can jump around here!"
said scratchy Mr. Ratchett.

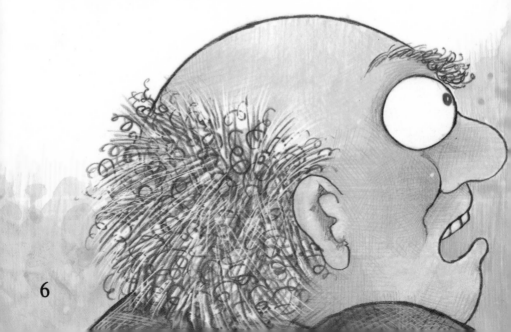

6

"They wanted to get away
from their scratchy neighbor,"
said the first man.

"Fiddle faddle!" cried Mr. Ratchett.
"There is nobody scratchy
around these parts."

Mr. Ratchett looked around him.
Sure enough,
there was no one scratchy
to be seen.

9

The moving van drove away.
Mr. Ratchett could hear
the moving men laughing
as they went down the road.

"Let them laugh!"
said Mr. Ratchett scratchily.

Everything was quiet.
Scratchy Mr. Ratchett
got on with his gardening.

"What lovely peace and quiet,"
he said in a cross voice.
He raked the soil.
He hoed around the cabbage.
"It's a bit too quiet,"
he grumbled to himself.
"Trust those Goats to go off
and have a good time.
They don't spare a thought
for the poor old man next door."

13

Up in the high hills,
the Goat family was jumping around.

"It's very quiet up here,"
said Father Goat.
He sounded rather sad.

"It's too quiet," said Mother Goat.

"There is no one to tease,"
said the little Goats sadly.

14

Back in his garden
scratchy Mr. Ratchett
sighed to himself,
"It's going to take me a long time
to get used to all this peace and quiet.
A man needs a bit of grumbling
to bring a sparkle to his eyes."

16

17

Rrrrm! Rrrrm! went something next door.

Scratchy Mr. Ratchett
looked over the fence.
The moving van was coming back again.

Out of it leaped the Goat family.
They carried their grandfather clock
inside the house.
Then they came back
for the television set.

"You again!" shouted Mr. Ratchett.
Under his grumpy garden clothes
his heart was singing for joy.

"We couldn't stay away!"
shouted the little Goats.
They began to butt and bleat
and make a tremendous noise.
"We like making trouble
and we need a scratchy neighbor
close by."

"Fiddle faddle!"
shouted scratchy Mr. Ratchett,
but he smiled as he said it.
What a lot of wonderful grumbling
he would be able to do tomorrow!

When the Goat family
couldn't see him,
he did a little grumbler's tap dance
in his grumpy gardening clothes and
his moaning boots . . .

. . . because he was so glad
that they were back.